WHICH PUPPY?

Kate Feiffer

Illustrated by Jules Feiffer

A Paula Wiseman Book
SIMON & SCHUSTER BOOKS FOR YOUNG READERS
New York • London • Toronto • Sydney

For Julie and Halley
—K. F.

For Maddy
—J. F.

SIMON & SCHUSTER BOOKS FOR YOUNG READERS
An imprint of Simon & Schuster Children's Publishing Division
1230 Avenue of the Americas, New York, New York 10020
Text copyright © 2009 by Kate Feiffer • Illustrations copyright © 2009 by Jules Feiffer
SIMON & SCHUSTER BOOKS FOR YOUNG READERS is a trademark of Simon & Schuster, Inc.
Book design by Lizzy Bromley • The text for this book is set in Vertrina.
The illustrations for this book are rendered in brush, ink, and watercolor markers.
Manufactured in the United States of America
2 4 6 8 10 9 7 5 3
Library of Congress Cataloging-in-Publication Data
Feiffer, Kate.
Which puppy? / Kate Feiffer ; illustrated by Jules Feiffer.
p. cm.
"A Paula Wiseman book."
Summary: Puppies from around the world—along with some would-be puppies—
compete with one another to become the First Family's new puppy.
ISBN: 978-1-4169-9147-2 (hardcover)
[1. Dogs—Fiction. 2. Animals—Infancy—Fiction. 3. White House (Washington, D.C.)—Fiction.
4. African Americans—Fiction. 5. Humorous stories.] I. Feiffer, Jules, ill. II. Title.
PZ7.F33346Wh 2009
[E]—dc22
2009002346

"Sasha and Malia,
I love you both more than you can imagine,
and you have earned the new puppy
that's coming with us to the White House."

–President Barack Obama during his speech on
November 4, 2008, the night he won the presidential election

The news about the puppy spread quickly.

Fireflies lit up with it immediately.

Geese quacked and yakked about it while flying
from New Hampshire to North Carolina.

A mule named Fred carried word down through the Grand Canyon.

Practically everyone knew by the time the sun set the next day.

The girls were getting a puppy.

What a lucky lucky lucky lucky lucky lucky lucky lucky lucky lucky lucky lucky

lucky lucky lucky puppy. Lucky lucky lucky lucky lucky lucky lucky. So lucky!

It seemed like almost everyone wanted to be that puppy.

That's right—everyone.

"And why not? I'd make a fine puppy," squeaked a guinea pig named Sam.

"I'm starting barking lessons tomorrow," bragged a turtle named Marple.

Keisha, a kitten, practiced begging, jumping up on people, and drooling. "I don't know why anyone would want a puppy instead of a kitten," she said. "But since they do, I'll pretend to be a puppy. How do I look?"

Of course, real puppies hoped to get chosen too.

Even puppies who lived in other countries thought they'd be perfect for the girls.

No one knew for sure what kind of puppy the girls wanted,
but everyone acted like they knew.

"They want a long puppy." "I say a shaggy puppy." "A tiny puppy, for sure." "A golden puppy." "It can't shed." "A giant puppy." "No pedigree." "It has to be friendly." "Must look gorgeous on TV." "It will have fancy whiskers." "It needs to have come from the school of hard knocks."

"We'll hold a contest to find the most presidential puppy in the country," announced the oldest Basset hound in Mississippi.

A week later, thousands of puppies, hundreds of reporters, and more kittens, skunks, turtles, raccoons, guinea pigs, and rabbits than can be counted on two hands gathered together.

The Basset hound proclaimed,
"First we'll race.
On your mark.
Get set.
Go!"

The puppies, and other animals
pretending to be puppies, leaped into
the air and flopped to the ground.

One by one, big puppy paws got
tangled together and they fumbled
and stumbled and tumbled.

(Keisha the kitten finished in the top ten.)

At the end of the race the Basset hound called out,
"Now we'll see who can bark the longest."

The puppies barked until their throats got sore.
(Marple the turtle could only get out three yelps.)

"The final event of the day will be a hoop jump," said the Basset hound.
He then lifted a hoop high into the air.

At the end of the day they had a winner.

The fastest, loudest puppy who could jump through the hoop was . . .

. . . fighting with another dog.

"No, no, no," howled
the Basset hound.
"This puppy won't
do at all."

A Neapolitan mastiff from Maryland spoke up. "Let lady luck lead the way with a lottery. Every pup in the place gets a ticket. The hound holding the winning number heads to Washington. Come one and come all. Get your number right here."

Puppies from the east and the west, the north and the south, and the middle of the country held tightly onto their tickets.

At the stroke of midnight the mastiff from Maryland picked a number out of a hat.

Amazingly the winner was . . .

. . . the mastiff from Maryland.

"Oh, will you look at this? It seems as if luck likes
this lady tonight, even though I'm no lady.
I'll see the rest of you old
dogs later. I'm heading
to Washington,"
he said.

"No, no, no," howled the Basset hound.
"This slick trickster is no
presidential pup."

A dog with a roly-poly body and long ears that stuck straight up in the air swaggered forward to the front of the large crowd and said,

"Ahem, excuse me, everyone, but ancient custom dictates that a true presidential puppy must have two rings around one paw, a heart on its face, an eye that winks, and a tail that tells time."

The puppies looked around. The reporters looked around. The kittens, skunks, turtles, raccoons, guinea pigs, and rabbits looked around.

They found a puppy with two rings around one paw. They spotted another puppy with a heart on its face and an eye that winks. And Sam, the guinea pig pretending to be a puppy, claimed that his tiny tail could tell time.

The old Basset hound from Mississippi tapped his paw on the ground and declared, "The girls will get three puppies instead of one."

So Sam the guinea pig,
the puppy with two rings
around one paw, and the puppy
with a heart on its face and an eye
that winked prepared to head to the
White House to become the next presidential pups.
They primped and packed and gave good-bye licks to their friends and family.

They arrived at the White House on a Saturday afternoon and scratched on the front door.

When the door opened, Sam and the two puppies stepped inside. They saw ceilings that reached to the sky, a red rug as long as a road, paintings of presidents on the walls, and . . .

. . . a puppy.

A puppy?

A PUPPY!!!!!!!!!!!!!

"Oh no!"

"This is terrible!"

"It can't be true!"

Sam and the two puppies turned around and, with their heads hung low, walked out the front door, down some stairs, and toward a fountain. They didn't get far at all before they heard voices.

"Where are you going?" called out the two girls who had just moved into the White House. "Won't you come back and play? We have a puppy who needs new friends."

So Sam the guinea pig, the puppy with two rings around one paw, and the puppy with a heart on its face and an eye that winked turned around and ran with the two girls back to the White House . . .

... where they played and played and played until no one could possibly play any longer.